THE AGE OF REVOLUTIONS
From AD1750 to AD1914

Dr Anne Millard

Illustrated by Joseph McEwan

Designed by Graham Round
Edited by Robyn Gee
Series editor Jenny Tyler

Contents

Picture Research: Penni O'Grady
Consultant Editors: Brian Adams, Verulamium Museum, St Albans, England; D. Barrass, University of East Anglia, England; Ben Burt, Museum of Mankind, London, England; T. R. Clayton, University of Cambridge, England; Dr M. Falkus, London School of Economics, England; Professor Norman Hampson, University of York, England; Peter Johnston, Commonwealth Institute, London, England; Dr Michael Loewe, University of Cambridge, England; Dr M. McCauley, University of London, England; Dr C. D. Sheldon, University of Cambridge, England; Dr R. Waller, University of Cambridge, England.
First published in 1979 by Usborne Publishing, Usborne House, 83-85 Saffron Hill, London EC1N 8RT. Copyright © 1990, 1979 Usborne Publishing Ltd. Printed in Belgium.

T 24855

A Revolution in Farming

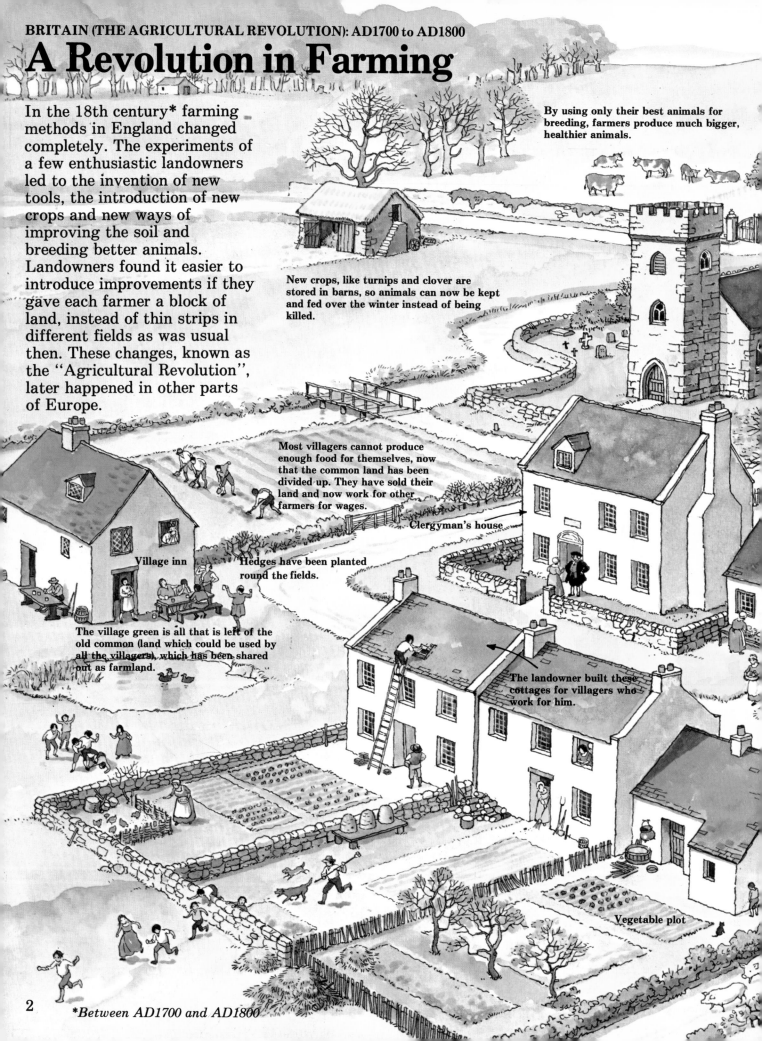

In the 18th century* farming methods in England changed completely. The experiments of a few enthusiastic landowners led to the invention of new tools, the introduction of new crops and new ways of improving the soil and breeding better animals. Landowners found it easier to introduce improvements if they gave each farmer a block of land, instead of thin strips in different fields as was usual then. These changes, known as the "Agricultural Revolution", later happened in other parts of Europe.

By using only their best animals for breeding, farmers produce much bigger, healthier animals.

New crops, like turnips and clover are stored in barns, so animals can now be kept and fed over the winter instead of being killed.

Most villagers cannot produce enough food for themselves, now that the common land has been divided up. They have sold their land and now work for other farmers for wages.

Clergyman's house

Village inn

Hedges have been planted round the fields.

The village green is all that is left of the old common (land which could be used by all the villagers), which has been shared out as farmland.

The landowner built these cottages for villagers who work for him.

Vegetable plot

2   *Between AD1700 and AD1800

Village windmill for grinding corn.

House of chief landowner of the village, often called the squire. Some other villagers own their land, but he still owns the most.

This carrier has just delivered some goods to the house.

New plough cuts deeper furrows.

Seed drill sows seeds in straight lines.

Doctor's house

Ditch for draining land that used to be too wet for growing crops.

Animal manure is spread on the land to make it more fertile.

Landowner (squire)

Blacksmith

This farmer owns the land he farms.

Village shop

This family is leaving to go and work in a town.

Milkmaid

Woman spinning

Landowner's wife

Hoeing keeps the crop free of weeds so there will be a bigger harvest.

This man rents a farm from the landowner.

In this field the farmer grows wheat one year, turnips the next, barley the third year and clover the fourth. This order of growing crops keeps the field fertile. Fields are no longer left unplanted every third year.

3

Machines and Factories

In the first half of the 18th century, most people in Britain still lived and worked in the countryside. Woollen and cotton cloth, produced in the north of England, were the chief manufactured goods. Before 1750 cloth was mainly made by hand, in people's homes. But by 1850 it was being made by machines in factories. The new factories employed lots of people and towns quickly grew up round them. These changes in working life have become known as the "Industrial Revolution".

Britain produced a great deal of woollen cloth. In the first half of the 18th century, most of it was made by villagers in their homes and sold to visiting merchants.

Then machines like this were invented. They helped spinners and weavers to work much faster. Later they were adapted to be driven by water, and later still by steam.

This is one of Watt's steam engines.

The early factories used water power to make their machines go. Various people experimented with the idea of using steam. Eventually a Scotsman called James Watt found out how to make steam engines drive the wheels of other machines and these were soon being used in factories.

This is an iron works. Iron was needed for making the new machines, but iron-smelting needed charcoal and the wood for making this was in short supply.

Coal was no good as its fumes made the iron brittle. Then, Abraham Darby discovered coal could be turned into coke which was pure enough for making iron.

People had been using coal to heat their homes for a long time, but it had been dug only from shallow mines. Deep mines were too dangerous.

Safety lamp

Several inventions made mining safer. The safety lamp cut down the danger of explosions. Steam pumps helped prevent flooding and there was also a machine which sucked out stale air.

Underground rails made it easier to haul coal to the surface from great depths, but conditions in the mines were still very bad. Small children were used to pull the heavy trucks.

The new machines were too big to fit into people's homes and too expensive for them to buy. Clever men with money to invest built factories like this one and bought machines to put in them. People working at home could not compete with the prices of factory-made goods, so they had to go and work in the factories. They were joined by country people who thought they would make a better living in the factories than on the land.

Drive-wheel transfers power from steam engine to spinning machines.

Leather belts attach drive-wheels to machines.

Factory owner showing visitors round.

Machines for spinning cotton.

Boy climbing into machine to mend it.

Exhausted children often fall asleep at work and are punished.

Women change the bobbins (reels) and watch for breaks in the thread.

Overseer

Machine-smashing

At first, conditions in the factories were very bad. Men, women and children worked very long hours for low wages. Machines had no safety guards and there were bad accidents.

Gradually laws were passed to make the factory owners improve conditions in the factories, make working hours shorter and protect the rights of working people.

Machines were very unpopular with people who had no jobs. Some people even banded together to smash them. One group was called the Luddites after their leader, Ned Ludd.

Life in the New Towns

Where factories were built, new towns quickly grew up to house the factory workers. They were overcrowded and unhealthy places and they caused many problems.

Factory owner's house

Factories

Railway (goods line)

Chimney sweep and apprentice

Policeman

Barrel organ

Hansom cab

Gas lamp

Pickpocket

Fruit-seller

Cheap houses, built back-to-back, were put up for the factory workers, especially in the northern towns. Often there were no toilets or running water. The streets were dirty and the air and rivers polluted by factories.

Diseases spread quickly. Until cheap ways of travelling were developed the workers had to live near the factories, which were often built near coal mines and ironworks.

6

1 The changes in farming and industry left some people without jobs and desperately poor. To get help they had to go and live in "workhouses". Conditions in the workhouses were very harsh to discourage lazy people from using them. Men and women lived in separate quarters so families were split up. Poor people often preferred to live on the streets.

2 Several reformers tried to help poor people. Dr Barnardo, shown here, set up children's homes and General Booth started a Christian organization called the Salvation Army.

3 Many laws were passed during the 19th century to improve people's lives by cleaning up towns, building better houses and setting up schools where all children could go without paying.

4 Old-age pensions started in 1909. These people are collecting theirs from the post office. In 1911, a law was passed which insured people against sickness and unemployment.

5 Workers began to join together to form trade unions so that they could bargain for better wages and working conditions by threatening to strike. At first the trade unions were illegal but gradually laws were passed which made them legal and gave them the right to picket (stand outside their work places and try to persuade other workers not to go in).

6 Some trade unionists and people who agreed with them formed the Labour Party. In the general election of 1906, 29 of their members were elected to parliament.

Transport and Travel

The Industrial Revolution brought about immense changes in transport and travel. Some important developments happened first in Britain, others happened first in America and other parts of Europe.

1

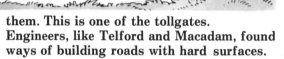

In England, companies called Turnpike Trusts were set up. They built and repaired roads and charged people tolls for using them. This is one of the tollgates. Engineers, like Telford and Macadam, found ways of building roads with hard surfaces.

2

New bridges were also built, many of them iron. This is the Clifton Suspension Bridge in England, designed by Brunel, a famous engineer.

3

Bicycles were in general use by the 1880s. The early "penny-farthings" were ridden by men, but later models were suitable for women to ride too.

4

As the population increased during the 19th century, cities grew in size. People had to live further from their work and horse-drawn buses were introduced to provide them with transport. Before long, city streets became packed with traffic.

5

The first motor cars were made in Germany in 1885. They remained too expensive for anyone but the very wealthy until the 1920s.

1 Canals

In the 18th century, it was much cheaper to send heavy goods by water than by road. Where there were no suitable rivers, canals were cut to link important ports and cities. Locks, like the ones shown here, took the boats up and down slopes. The barges were pulled by horses walking along the "towpath."

2

In 1869 the Suez Canal, which links the Mediterranean Sea to the Red Sea, was opened. This canal cut several weeks off the journey from Europe to India. Later, in 1915, another long ship canal was opened. This was the Panama Canal in Central America which joined the Atlantic and Pacific Oceans.

Railways

Early type of locomotive designed by famous railway engineer, George Stephenson.

The first steam locomotive to run on rails was built in England in 1804 by Richard Trevithick. Twenty years later, the first passenger railway was opened and from then on railways became very popular. They were a quick, cheap and safe way of carrying people and goods. As train services improved, it became possible for ordinary people to go on seaside and country holidays. England's roads and canals were neglected.

London got its first long stretch of underground railway in 1863. Until 1890, when electric trains came in, the underground trains were steam-powered. The tunnels are still filled with the soot they made.

1 Sea travel

2

3

Very fast sailing ships called "clippers" were built during the 19th century and used to carry light cargoes such as tea. A completely new kind of ship was also being developed at this time. These ships were built of iron and had steam-engines. They gradually replaced sailing ships.

Many lighthouses were built and a life-boat service introduced, making sea travel much safer than it had been in the past.

Faster and safer sea travel tempted wealthy people to take holidays abroad. In 1869, Thomas Cook ran his first holiday tour to Egypt.

1 The first flights

2

The French Montgolfier brothers were the first people to take off into the air. This was in 1783 in a hot-air balloon. Other balloonists tried using hydrogen.

At the beginning of the 20th century, two Americans, the Wright brothers, built a glider like this one. Later they built an aeroplane fitted with an engine and in 1903 made the first powered flight.

Key dates

AD1663/1770	Turnpike trusts set up.
AD1783	First ascent of hot air balloon.
AD1804	First steam vehicle to run on rails.
AD1829	First railroads opened in U.S.A.
AD1839	First pedal bicycle made.
AD1863	Opening of first underground railway.
AD1869	Suez Canal opened.
AD1885	**Karl Benz** made a 3-wheeled motor car.
AD1886	**Gottlieb Daimler** made a 4-wheeled motor car.
AD1903	First powered flight.

9

French Revolution and Napoleon's Wars

1 The King of France, Louis XVI, and his wife, Marie Antoinette, lived in the magnificent palace of Versailles near Paris. Here they were surrounded by rich nobles who hardly paid any taxes. Louis was not a good ruler and they were all unpopular with the people.

2 Many nobles were very arrogant and treated everyone else with scorn. The middle classes were very annoyed by this.

3 The peasants had to pay taxes to the church, the government and their local lord. They also had to work for their lords.

4 By 1789, the government had no more money left, so the king was forced to call a meeting of the States General (parliament), which had not met for 175 years. Later the States General passed many reforms but most people were still not satisfied.

5 On July 14, 1789, a crowd in Paris captured a royal prison called the Bastille. This sparked off riots all over France.

6 The revolution became more violent. The king, queen, nobles and anyone not revolutionary enough were executed by guillotine.

7 European rulers were horrified by events in France and soon the French were at war with most of the rest of Europe. Here a soldier is recruiting people for the French army. Many clever young officers were found, in particular Napoleon Bonaparte.

8 Napoleon was so successful as a military commander that he became First Consul of France and then had himself crowned Emperor.

9 Napoleon gained control of much of Europe. He made his brothers and sisters rulers of the lands he conquered. This map shows the lands ruled by him and members of his family by 1810.

10

Napoleon planned to invade Britain, his most determined enemy. But after the British defeated the French at sea in the Battle of Trafalgar, he gave up the idea.

11

In 1812, Napoleon invaded Russia with an army of 600,000 men. He defeated the Tsar's army and marched to Moscow. But the Russians had set fire to Moscow and removed all the provisions. Here the French army is returning home in the middle of winter. Hundreds of thousands of them died from cold and hunger.

12

After his disastrous invasion of Russia, there was a general reaction against Napoleon in Europe. British troops helped the Spanish to drive the French out of Spain.

The Battle of Waterloo

The Battle of Waterloo was the last great battle in the wars against Napoleon. The French were completely defeated by a British army, led by Wellington, and a Prussian army, led by Blücher.

Louis XVIII was made King of France, and Napoleon was imprisoned on the small British island of St Helena in the South Atlantic Ocean, where he died in 1821.

Key dates	
AD1789	First meeting of the States General.
AD1792	France went to war with Austria and Prussia.
AD1793/1794	Period called "The Reign of Terror". Hundreds of people guillotined.
AD1804	**Napoleon** became Emperor.
AD1805	Battle of Trafalgar.
AD1808/1814	War between the British and French in Spain and Portugal.
AD1812	**Napoleon's** invasion of Russia.
AD1815	Battle of Waterloo.

New Nations and Ways of Governing

The 18th and 19th centuries were times of great change in the way countries were governed.

There were many revolutions and several new, independent nations emerged.

1 Independence for America

In 1775 war broke out. The British Army were far from home and supplies. The colonists were on their own ground and their riflemen were very good shots.

In 1781 the British surrendered at Yorktown and in 1783 they signed a treaty recognizing the United States of America as an independent nation.

Most European settlers in America lived in the 13 colonies* on the east coast. In the early 18th century Britain helped them in their wars against the Indians and the French. The British then taxed them to pay for the wars. The colonists hated the taxes and sometimes attacked British tax officers.

When the new constitution (set of rules by which a country is governed) had been agreed upon, George Washington was chosen as first President of America.

Key Dates

AD1775/1783 War of American Independence.
AD1789/1797 **George Washington** President of the U.S.A.
AD1818/1883 Life of **Karl Marx**.
AD1859/1860 **General Garibaldi** drove French and Austrians out of Italy.
AD1861 Kingdom of Italy founded.
AD1871 German Empire founded. **William I** became Kaiser and **Bismarck** First Chancellor.

Germany

Early in the 19th century Germany was a group of states, the strongest of which was Prussia. In 1861 William I became King of Prussia. With his chief minister, Bismarck, he gradually brought all Germany under his control. In 1871 William was proclaimed Kaiser (emperor) of Germany.

Battleship being launched

Germany became one of the strongest countries in Europe. It quickly built a large navy, developed its industries and won colonies in Africa and the Far East.

Germans became very interested in their country's history. The operas of Wagner based on tales of German gods and heroes, became very popular.

*A colony is a settlement ruled by the country from which the settlers have come.

Italy

In Italy, some states were independent, some were ruled by France and some by Austria. General Garibaldi and his soldiers, known as the "Red Shirts" (above) helped to drive the foreigners out of Italy and make it an independent nation.

ITALY IN 1866

GERMAN EMPIRE IN 1871

1 Ideas about government

In Britain, the people chose which political party should rule by voting at elections. At first few people had the right to vote but gradually it was extended to all men.

2

Some women began to demand the vote. They were called suffragettes.

They held marches and caused as much disturbance as possible to win support.

3

Rulers in many countries were afraid of democracy (people having a say in the running of the country). Soldiers were used against the people who protested.

4

People with revolutionary ideas were sometimes executed or put in prison so they could not lead the people against their ruler.

5

Some people believed any form of government was wrong. They were called anarchists and they killed many political leaders.

6

A German thinker, called Karl Marx, wrote many books with new ideas about government. He wanted people to get rid of their rulers in a revolution and then have new governments run by the working people. Communism is based on his ideas.

Slavery and Civil War

In the southern states of the United States of America there were large plantations. Since the 17th century the plantation owners had bought slaves from Africa to work for them. The northern states had small farms and industries and did not need slaves.

NORTHERN (UNION) STATES

SOUTHERN (CONFEDERATE) STATES

The slave trade became well organized. Europeans either captured Africans or bought them from local rulers, like the King of Dahomey, shown here.

Conditions on the ships carrying the slaves to America were dreadful as the more slaves a trader could get on a ship, the greater his profit.

When they reached America, the slaves who had survived the voyage were sold at auctions. They could be sold again at any time and families were often parted.

Some slaves were lucky enough to work in their master's house but most were used as field hands on the plantation. Most estate owners grew either cotton, tobacco or sugar, all of which need constant attention. Because of the heat African slaves were thought best for this work. Some masters were very cruel but others treated their slaves quite well.

Many slaves tried to escape to the north where they would be free as there was no slavery. A black woman called Harriet Tubman, helped 19 groups of slaves escape.

AM I NOT A MAN AND A BROTHER?

Protests against slavery began to grow. In 1833 slavery was abolished in the British Empire and the Anti-Slavery Society was founded in America. This is its badge.

In the American Congress (parliament) there were bitter arguments about slavery. The northerners wanted to abolish it but the southerners were determined to keep slaves.

The outbreak of war

In 1861 the southern states elected their own president and broke away from the Union of the United States, declaring themselves a "confederacy". The north thought the states should stay united so war broke out between the Unionists (northerners) and Confederates (southerners). It lasted for four years. There were many fierce battles and nearly 635,000 people lost their lives.

Camp

Mine exploding

Southern (Confederate) flag

Northern (Unionist) flag

Barbed wire

Trench

A new style of fighting developed during the American Civil War. Soldiers made trenches protected by barbed wire. They used mines, hand-grenades and flame throwers.

At first the southerners, led by General Lee, were quite successful. But the north had more soldiers, factories to make weapons and railways to transport them. It used its navy to stop ships bringing supplies to the south. Despite terrible suffering the southerners fought bravely on, but in 1865 they were finally forced to surrender.

1 After the war

President Abraham Lincoln, who had been elected before the war broke out, hoped to make a lasting peace but he was assassinated at Ford's Theater in Washington.

2

The south had been ruined by the war and its main town, Richmond, had been burned. For years afterwards both white and black people were very poor.

3

Some southerners still regarded black people as slaves. They formed a secret society called the Ku Klux Klan. Members covered themselves in sheets and terrorized black people.

Explorers and Empire Builders

In 1750 there were still huge areas of the world where Europeans had never been. During the 19th and late 18th centuries European explorers set out to discover as much as they could about the lands and oceans of the world. Traders and settlers followed and the European countries began to set up colonies abroad which they ruled.

Captain Cook

Captain Cook led three expeditions (1768-79) to the Pacific Ocean. He visited islands such as Tahiti where he was met by war canoes.

He explored the east coast of Australia. Its strange animals fascinated the artists and scientists on the expedition.

He also sailed round the islands of New Zealand. The crew of his ship *Endeavour* landed and met the Maoris who lived there.

1 Exploring Africa

During the 19th century people began to explore and make maps of Africa. They saw wonderful sights such as the Victoria Falls, but many fell ill and died of strange diseases.

2 On a journey in search of the source of the Nile, two British explorers, Speke and Grant, stayed with Mutesa, King of Buganda, who treated them with great hospitality.

3 Some explorers, such as Dr Livingstone, were also Christian missionaries.* Missionaries set up hospitals and schools for the Africans, as well as churches.

4 The Frenchman, René Caillé, was one of the earliest European explorers in the Sahara Desert. He was also one of the first Europeans to see the ancient African city of Timbuktu.

5 There were also several women explorers in the 19th century. This is Alexandrine Tinné, a wealthy Dutch heiress, who travelled through much of North Africa and the Sudan.

16   *People who went to foreign lands to teach the people about Christianity.*

Other expeditions

1

Richard Burton was a daring explorer. He disguised himself to visit the Arab holy city, Mecca, where only Muslims were allowed.

2

Many explorers never returned from the jungles of South America where they went to make maps and search for lost cities.

3

Later explorers travelled to the frozen north and south. In 1909, Robert Peary, an American, was the first to reach the North Pole. Roald Amundsen reached the South Pole in 1911.

Setting up colonies

1

Europeans wanted new places to sell their factory-made goods. They also wanted to buy raw materials such as cotton and tea.

2

If quarrels between local rulers threatened trade, the Europeans sent armies. These often stayed after the fighting was over.

3

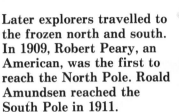

They also sent officials to organize and govern the territory for them, thus setting up a colony there.

4

More and more Europeans went to the colonies and settled there with their families. They organized vast estates where the local people worked and grew tea, rubber, cotton and foodstuffs or reared sheep and cattle. Later, when minerals were discovered, factories and railways were built and still more people went to live in the colonies.

5

In Europe, politicians were worried by the increase in population and they encouraged people to go and settle in the colonies where there was land and work for them.

17

Europeans in Africa

1 North Africa

In the early 19th century most of the countries of North Africa were part of the Ottoman Empire*. But the Ottoman Empire was breaking up and European powers began to move in.

The French gained control of Algeria and later Tunisia and Morocco. Here, desert tribesmen are attacking one of the French forts, which is defended by the famous French Foreign Legion.

2

The ruler of Egypt needed money, so he sold his shares in the Suez Canal to Britain. Britain became involved in Egyptian affairs and later took over the government.

3

Egypt also ruled the Sudan. In 1883 a religious leader, the Mahdi, led a revolt. Britain sent an army led by General Gordon, but it was defeated at Khartoum.

Trading in the West

These gold objects were made by the Ashanti, a people who live in west Africa. They grew rich by trading in gold and slaves. They fought the British in several wars and were defeated in 1901.

Zimbabwe

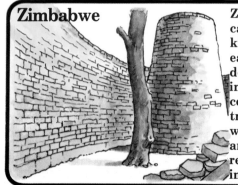

Zimbabwe was the capital city of a rich kingdom in south-east Africa. It was destroyed probably in the early 19th century by rival tribes. The people were clever builders and this is the remains of a temple in the city.

*Empire of Muslim people from Middle East called the Ottoman Turks.

1 South Africa

Cecil Rhodes

Dutch settlers had first arrived in South Africa in 1652. They set up Cape Colony on the Cape of Good Hope. Most of them were farmers and they became known as "Boers" (Dutch word for farmers). In 1814 an international treaty gave Cape Colony to the British. The Boers hated being ruled by the British and between 1835 and 1837 many of them set off northwards, with all their possessions in wagons, to find new lands free from British rule. This movement is called the "Great Trek".

Cecil Rhodes made a fortune from diamond and gold mines, then formed a company to build a railway from the British colony to the mining area north of the Boer states. In 1895 this area became known as Rhodesia.

The Grab for Africa

- FRENCH
- BRITISH
- GERMAN
- PORTUGUESE
- BELGIAN
- SPANISH
- ITALIAN

In 1880 much of Africa was still independent of any European country. Between 1880 and the outbreak of World War I in 1914, the European powers carved up nearly the whole of Africa between them. This map shows Africa in 1914.

The Boers came into conflict with the Zulus, the fiercest of the neighbouring African tribes. The British helped the Boers and eventually, in 1879, the Zulus were completely defeated.

The British gradually increased their control over the Boer states. In 1886, gold was discovered in one of them and many more British people came out to work in them.

In 1899 war broke out between the Boers and the British. The Boers did very well at first. They rode fast horses, were good at stalking the enemy and knew the countryside.

The British destroyed the Boers' farms and animals and put all the Boers they could find, including women and children, into special prison camps. In 1902 the Boers surrendered.

Key dates

AD1814	Britain gained control of Cape Colony.
c. AD1830	Collapse of Kingdom of Zimbabwe.
AD1830	French began to take over North Africa.
AD1835/1837	The Great Trek.
AD1875	Britain bought Egypt's shares in the Suez Canal.
AD1878/9	Zulu War.
AD1885	Fall of Khartoum.
AD1896	Britain took over Matabeleland which became Rhodesia.
AD1899/1902	Boer War.
AD1901	Ashanti kingdom became British.
AD1910	Union of South Africa set up.

The British in India

1

This is a court of the British East India Company which started as a trading company. By the 19th century it governed most of India.

2

The British built railways and schools and tried to modernize India. They also tried to stop some of the Indians' religious customs. The Indians resented this interference. In 1857 some *sepoys* (Indian soldiers in the British Army) mutinied and the revolt quickly spread. The British eventually regained control but in future changes were made more carefully.

3

After the Mutiny the East India Company lost its right to rule and the British Government appointed its own officials. Indian princes also lost their power but were very wealthy and still lived in great luxury.

4

Queen Victoria became Empress of India in 1876. Many Indians felt this created a special tie with Britain and the royal family often went to India.

5

The British brought their own customs and entertainments to India. They introduced cricket which became one of the national sports of India.

6

Most Indians were very poor. The cities were crowded and outbreaks of disease and famines were common. Improvements could be made only slowly.

7

The two main religious groups in India were the Hindus and the Muslims. They were rivals and sometimes there were riots and people were killed.

8

The Indians had little say in how their country was ruled so a group of them formed the National Congress. At first they just wanted reforms but later they began to demand independence from Britain.

Convicts and Settlers

1

In 1788 the British Government began to send criminals to Australia as a punishment. Many stayed on there after they had served their sentence.

2

Soon many other settlers arrived. Most of them wanted land where they could raise sheep and cattle. Some went in search of gold and minerals.

3

Life in Australia in the 19th century was hard and often dangerous. There were "bushrangers" (outlaws). The most famous was Ned Kelly.

4

As more settlers arrived they took land from the Aborigines (native Australians), many of whom were killed, or died of diseases brought by settlers.

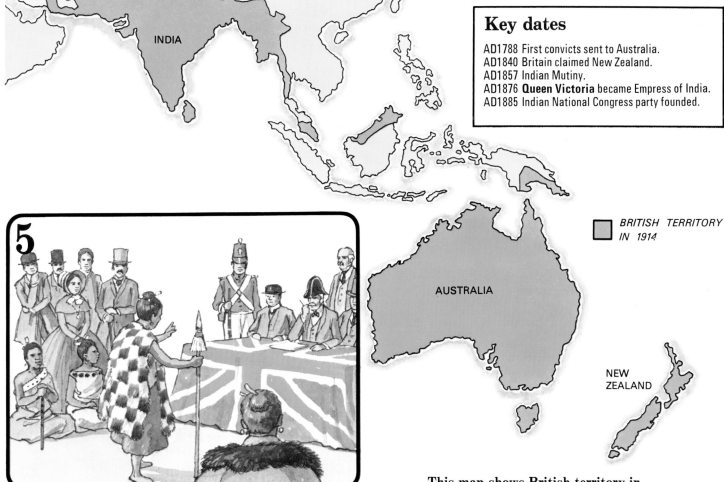

Key dates

AD1788 First convicts sent to Australia.
AD1840 Britain claimed New Zealand.
AD1857 Indian Mutiny.
AD1876 **Queen Victoria** became Empress of India.
AD1885 Indian National Congress party founded.

INDIA

BRITISH TERRITORY IN 1914

AUSTRALIA

NEW ZEALAND

5

European settlers first arrived in New Zealand in the 1790s. In 1840 the British Government took over the country. The Governor and the Maori chiefs made a treaty agreeing how much land the settlers could have, but this did not prevent fierce wars between the Maoris and the settlers.

This map shows British territory in India, South-East Asia, and Australia in 1914. By this time Australia and New Zealand had gained the right to rule themselves but they were still part of the British Empire.

Indians and Settlers

Many tribes of Indians lived in North America, each with its own way of life and language. The Indians of the Great Plains lived by farming until they captured horses from the Spaniards in the 16th century. Then most of them became nomads, hunting buffalo across the Plains and rearing horses. They lived like this for about 200 years until European settlers moved west and took the Indians' hunting grounds for their farms.

Tepee (tent made of buffalo hide)

Buffalo hunt. The buffalo provided Indians with food, clothing and shelter.

Chiefs

Traders

Meat drying

Travois (sledge)

We have removed part of this tepee wall so you can see inside.

Preparing buffalo hide

Medicine man

The Plains Indians lived in tepees which could be packed up when the buffalo moved on. The first white men to meet the Indians were traders who sold metal goods, blankets and guns and bought buffalo hides and horses.

1 Settlers move west

As more settlers from Europe moved into the original 13 States of the United States of America, more land was needed. In 1803 the Americans bought Louisiana from the French.

Settlers began to cross the Appalachian Mountains and the Great Plains, looking for land to farm. They travelled with wagons packed with everything they needed for their new homes, so most people, except for guards and cattle herders had to walk. It usually took many months to reach a suitable area.

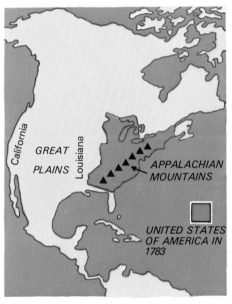

2 The settlers made treaties with the Indians promising not to take all their land. But the treaties were soon broken when settlers wanted more land.

3 In 1848 gold was discovered in California. Thousands of people flocked there in the "goldrush" hoping to make fortunes.

4 Railways were built to link the east and west coasts. These brought more settlers to the Great Plains, leaving less and less land for the Indians.

5 The men who built the tracks had to be fed. They employed hunters armed with rifles who killed most of the buffalo on which the Indians had depended.

6 The Indians fought the settlers. The wars were bitter and both sides were cruel. The Indians won victories such as at Little Big Horn when they killed General Custer and his men. But the settlers had more soldiers and better weapons and many Indian tribes were almost wiped out.

7 The Indians were left with only small areas of land called reservations. They were controlled by government agents and most were very unhappy.

The Wild West

In the United States of America, many of the people who moved westwards to the vast plains and prairies started raising cattle or growing corn. Towns, like this one, grew up to supply their needs. At first they were wild, lawless places, especially when cowboys from the ranches came into town. They brought great herds of cattle to the railway depots from which they were taken to feed the people in the cities.

Large industries and cities like New York and Chicago grew up. The first skyscrapers were built. By 1890 the United States was one of the world's most powerful industrial nations.

At first life was hard for the farmers on the plains, but soon they started using tougher crops and steel ploughs and later bought machines for harvesting and threshing. Before long they were producing vast quantities of grain which were sold all over the world.

From all over Europe poor people and people persecuted for their ideas came to the United States to start a new life. Some were lucky, but many of them ended up working in factories and living in hard conditions in the big cities.

24

New Countries in South America

1 Between 1810 and 1825 a series of revolutions ended the rule of Spain and Portugal in South America and set up 11 new states. This is Simon Bolivar, one of the revolutionary leaders who helped to achieve this.

2 Coffee was brought from Arabia to South America and grown on large estates. By 1860 it was the main export of many states.

3 Another important export was rubber. It was made from the juice of trees growing in the Amazon jungle.

4 Many of the Indian tribes in the Amazon jungle attacked the white men who came to take over their lands.

5 On the vast pampas (grasslands) of the southeast, there were huge ranches where great herds of cattle were reared by cowboys called "gauchos".

The cattle were used for making canned meat which was sold abroad.

1 Mexico

1 Mexicans and Americans were always quarrelling about who should control Texas. It belonged to Mexico but many Americans had settled there and wanted to be part of the United States. Here Davy Crockett and a group of other Americans are defending the Alamo Fort against a Mexican attack.

2 In 1863 the European powers, led by France, tried to get control of Mexico by making Archduke Maximilian of Austria, Emperor of Mexico. In 1867 the Mexicans shot him.

3 From 1867 onwards the Mexicans ruled themselves. In the early 20th century civil war broke out. One of the revolutionary leaders was Pancho Villa, shown here.

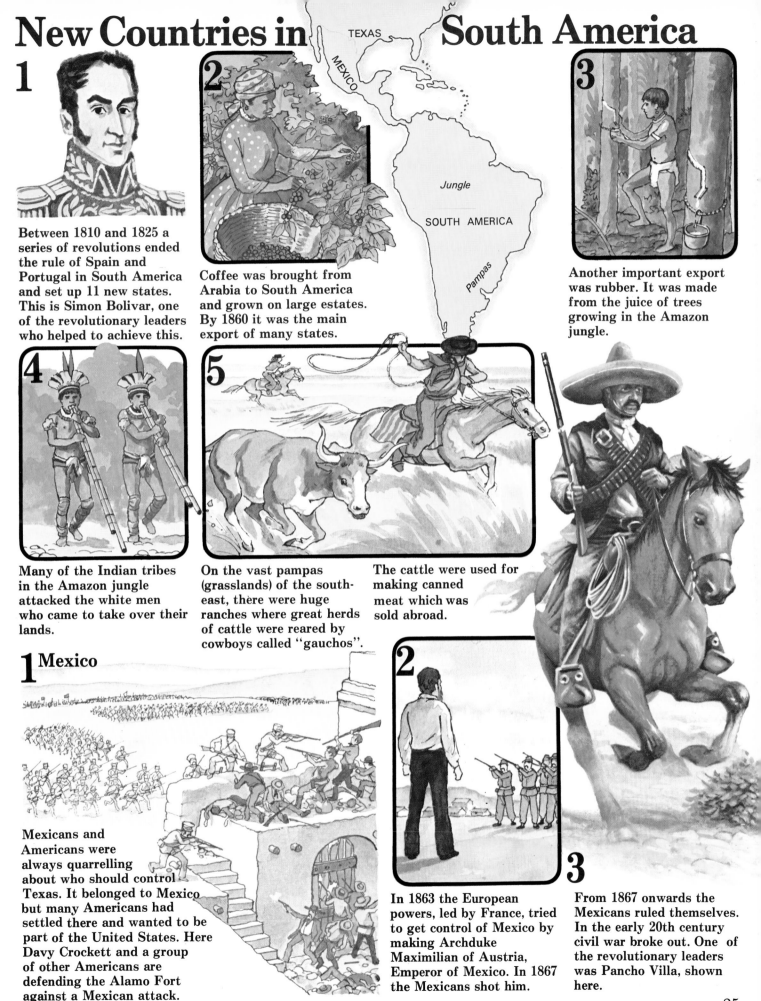

Life Under the Tsars

1

The Tsars (emperors) of Russia governed their huge country from St Petersburg. There was no parliament and the Tsars and nobles, from whom they chose their ministers and officials, were very cut off from the rest of the country. Much of their time was spent at balls and receptions.

2

Most Russians were members of the Orthodox Christian Church, which supported the idea that the Tsar was chosen by God and that he alone had the right to rule.

3

Talking or writing about government reforms was forbidden. Secret police tracked down anyone suspected of wanting to change the government.

4

Many people who criticized the government for its inefficiency and cruelty, were executed or sent into exile in a part of Russia called Siberia.

5

During the 19th century there were several great novelists, playwrights and composers at work in Russia. The Russian ballet became world-famous.

6

Many Russians were serfs—peasants who lived on nobles' estates and were treated as slaves. Serfs could be bought and sold. They had to do any work their estate owner demanded and they were often given cruel punishments for small mistakes. There were frequent uprisings and riots. Eventually, in 1861, Tsar Alexander II freed the serfs. The government lent them money to buy land, but they were too poor to buy farming equipment and pay back the loans. Their lives were not much improved and some were even worse off than before.

The Crimean War

The Russians wanted to expand their empire. In the late 18th and early 19th centuries they expanded eastwards. They also won land around the Black Sea, by helping the people of these territories free themselves from the Turkish Empire. The countries of Europe were suspicious of Russia's ambitions. In 1853 Britain and France tried to capture the area called the Crimea, to stop Russian expansion. One incident in this war was the Charge of the Light Brigade (shown here). A British force misunderstood an order and charged the Russian guns.

1 Discontent grows

This is Nicholas II, who became Tsar in 1894. He was a well-meaning and kind man but he was not strong enough to be a good ruler.

2

Nicholas's wife, Alexandra, was under the spell of a monk called Rasputin. She believed he could cure her son of a blood disease, but others thought him evil.

3

Factories and industrial towns were growing up in Russia. Living conditions in the towns were very bad and many people started demanding changes.

4

In 1905 a crowd of workers went on strike and marched to the Tsar's palace to tell him their problems. Soldiers, fearing a revolution, fired on them.

5

The Tsar allowed a *Duma* (parliament) to meet for a while but then dismissed it. Meanwhile, a group of people in exile, led by Lenin, were planning a revolution.

Key dates

AD1762/1796	Reign of **Catherine the Great**.
AD1812	Invasion of Russia by Napoleon.
AD1853/1856	Crimean War.
AD1855/1881	Reign of **Alexander II**.
AD1861	Serfs freed.
AD1894/1917	Reign of **Nicholas II**.
AD1904/1905	Russia defeated in war with Japan.
AD1905	Massacre of strikers outside Tsar's palace.
AD1906	Meeting of Duma (parliament).

Western Ideas in the East

Japan

From about 1640 onwards Japan had no contact with the countries of the west, except for a few Dutch traders. Then, in 1853, Commodore Perry, the commander of a squadron of American warships, sailed to Japan and got permission for America to trade with Japan. Soon European powers followed and Japan made trade agreements with many European countries.

It was hundreds of years since any emperor of Japan had had any real power. An official called the Shogun ruled the country for the emperor. This is the last Shogun of Japan.

In 1868 the 15-year-old Emperor left the old capital, Kyoto, and set up a new one in Edo (Tokyo). Here he is arriving in Edo, where he took back power from the Shogun and set up a western-style parliament.

The small picture above shows the opening of the first parliament.

The Samurai (warriors) were replaced by a new army, trained in modern methods of fighting by advisers from France and Germany.

The Japanese learnt many other things from the west. They built railways and factories and started producing large numbers of goods quickly and cheaply.

The Japanese wanted to win power overseas. They started to interfere in China and Korea. This made them rivals with the Russians and in 1904 Japan and Russia went to war. The new, efficient Japanese army and navy quickly defeated the Russians.

1 China

Between 1644 and 1912, China was ruled by the Ch'ing (also called the Manchu) Emperors. One of the greatest was Ch'ien Lung (1736-95), shown here.

2

The Ch'ing emperors fought many wars to protect their frontiers, win more territory and put down rebellions. At first they were successful but the wars were very expensive and later emperors found it more and more difficult to pay for them. The country slowly became weaker.

3

The Chinese population was growing quickly but farming methods were still very old-fashioned. It was difficult to grow enough food for everyone.

4

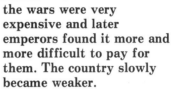

The Chinese Government did not like foreigners and allowed them to trade only in certain areas. The British were keen to extend these areas and in 1839 they went to war.

5

The British won the war in 1842. They forced the Chinese to sign a treaty which gave them Hong Kong and allowed them to trade in certain other ports.

6

Some Chinese decided to strengthen China by adopting certain Western ideas and inventions, such as railways, and steamships. But many still hated foreign ideas.

7

People who hated foreigners formed a secret society called the "Boxers". In 1900 they started attacking all the foreigners they could find in China. Here they are storming a foreign embassy.

8

This is the Empress Tzu Hsi. From 1862 to 1908 she ruled China, first for her son, then for her nephew. She often plotted with those who hated foreigners.

9

In 1911 there was a revolution and the last Ch'ing Emperor was expelled from China. This is Sun Yat-sen the first President of China.

Time Chart:
Ideas and Inventions

Agriculture and Industry

Transport and Travel

AD1750

Introduction of new crops and selective breeding of farm animals in Britain.

John Kay invented the "flying shuttle" for weaving cloth (1733).

 James Hargreaves invented the "spinning jenny" for spinning thread (1764).

Richard Arkwright invented a water-driven spinning machine (1769).

AD1770

Great age of canal building in Europe.

 James Watt invented a steam engine which could drive machines like the power-loom (1782).

Samuel Crompton invented the "spinning-mule" (1784).

 First cast-iron bridge. Built by **Abraham Darby**, at Ironbridge in England (1779).

AD1790

First steam vehicle to run on rails. Built by **Richard Trevithick** (1804).

AD1810

First power-driven printing press introduced (1810).

Safety lamp for miners invented by **Sir Humphrey Davy** (1813).

Electric motor and generator invented by Michael Faraday (1821).

 First steam ship crossed the Atlantic (1819).

Opening of Stockton to Darlington Railway, the first successful passenger railway system (1825).

Railway engineer, **George Stephenson**, built his train, the "Rocket" (1829).

AD1830

 Beginning of commercial manufacture of machine for reaping corn, invented by **Cyrus H. McCormick** (1840).

First pedal bicycles manufactured.

AD1850

 Barbed wire invented. First used in U.S.A.

Steam plough in use.

First oil well drilled. Titusville, Pennsylvania, U.S.A. (1859).

Combine Harvester invented. Developed first in U.S.A. After 1914 used in Europe.

Building began in London on the world's first underground railway system (1863).

Union Pacific and Central Pacific Railroads met to become the first line across the American continent (1869).

Opening of the Suez Canal (1869).

First electric tram opened (1874).

First oil tanker built (1878).

AD1870

Sir Charles Parsons invented the steam turbine which made ships faster and created very powerful pumps.

Development of successful electric motors.

 Karl Benz made a 3-wheeled motor car (1885).

Gottlieb Daimler made a 4-wheeled motor car.

Pneumatic tyre invented by **John B. Dunlop** (1888).

Building began on the Trans-Siberian Railway (1891).

AD1890

Ford Motor Company founded (1903).

 The Wright brothers made the first powered aeroplane flight (1903).

Louis Blériot made the first flight across the English Channel (1909).

AD1910

Beginning of conveyor belt mass production in the United States of America.

Diesel-electric railway engines first used (1913).

Medicine

Other Inventions

First vaccinations. **Edward Jenner** vaccinated people against smallpox.

First electric battery. Made by **Alessandro Volta** (1800).

Gas-lighting first in use.

William Fox-Talbot introduced the first camera to take photographic negatives.

Telegraph first in use (1837).

Morse code invented by **Samuel Morse** and adopted as the telegraphic code.

Florence Nightingale improved hospitals and nursing in England.

The **Red Cross** (an international medical and welfare organization) was founded (1864).

Louis Pasteur worked on killing germs in food.

First practical domestic sewing machine invented by **Isaac M. Singer,** Boston, U.S.A. (1851).

First telegraph cable laid across the Atlantic Ocean (1866).

Robert Koch worked to eliminate tuberculosis and cholera.

Joseph Lister began the practice of using antiseptics during operations.

Marie Curie discovered the radium cure for diseases.

The Remington Company began making typewriters (1873).

Telephone invented by **Alexander Graham Bell** (1876).

First gramophone made by **Thomas Edison.**

Marconi invented the wireless (1895).

First public motion picture show (Paris, 1895).

First vacuum cleaners in use.

Index

Going Further

Books to read

If you look in a library or bookshop, you will find lots of books about this period of history. Here are a few of the interesting ones.
The Old Regime and the Revolution, Power for the People, The War of American Independence and *Transported to Van Diemen's Land*—4 books in the Cambridge Introduction to the History of Mankind (Cambridge University Press).
Honest Rogues: The Inside Story of Smuggling by Harry T. Sutton (Batsford-Heritage).
Freedom and Revolution and *Age of Machines* by R. J. Unstead (Macdonald).
Ishi: Last of his Tribe by Theodore Kroeber (Puffin).
Underground to Canada by Barbara C. Smucker (Puffin).
Children on the Oregon Trail by A. Rutgers Van Der Loeff (Puffin).
Escape from France by Ronald Welch (Puffin).
Castors Away! by Hester Burton (Puffin).

*These books are novels.

Places to visit

There are lots of places where you can see things from this period of history. Most museums have furniture, costumes, weapons and everyday objects in their collections. You can find out about museums all over Britain from a booklet called *Museums and Galleries* (British Leisure Publications), which you can buy in newsagents and bookshops.

Paintings can tell you a lot about this period too. They often show the clothes and houses of the people who had them painted. Look in art galleries and at art books in libraries.

Look out for great houses and houses once lived in by famous people. Some of these and other interesting historical places are listed in *History Around Us* by Nathaniel Harrie (Hamlyn). UE